Written by Lauren Clauss
Illustrated by the Disney Storybook Art Team

𝒟isnℯℽ PRESS

Los Angeles • New York

ISBN 978-1-368-02789-2

FAC-029261-18138

Library of Congress Control Number: 2018935467

Manufactured in the United States of America

For more Disney Press fun, visit www.disneybooks.com

SUSTAINABLE
FORESTRY
INITIATIVE

Certified Sourcing

www.sfiprogram.org
SFI-01415

Huey, Dewey, and Louie were so excited. The first day of school was coming up! They couldn't wait to visit their uncle Donald. He had promised to help them get ready.

When they arrived, Mickey, Minnie, and Goofy were already there.
The whole gang was going to help!

"Are you boys ready for the first day?" Mickey asked.

"Do you have your backpacks packed?" Minnie added.

"We're not ready at all!" Dewey told them.
"We don't even know what we *should* have!" Huey said.

Goofy, Donald, and Mickey shared nervous looks as the nephews ran off
to gather supplies.

"Is this what we're supposed to bring?" Louie asked after grabbing everything he thought they'd need . . . including camping gear.

Donald couldn't believe it. "Boys, we've got a lot of work to do."

"Let's start with my favorite school supply," Mickey said. "Snacks!"
Mickey and the gang took Donald's nephews to the grocery store and picked out some healthy snacks.

Donald, Goofy, Daisy, and Minnie gathered even more school supplies for Huey, Dewey, and Louie at the store.

"Gawrsh, I wish it was my first day of school again," Goofy said.

"Me too!" Daisy chimed in.

When Donald's nephews and the gang got home, it was time to pack their backpacks.

"More stickers in my backpack, please!" Huey shouted.

"Can I have some apple slices, Minnie?" Dewey asked.

"Don't forget the glue sticks . . . oh, and the tissues . . . and my new pencils!" Louie cheered.

The next morning, the nephews got up bright and early for their first day of school. Their backpacks were stuffed, their snacks were packed, and Huey, Dewey, and Louie were excited about what the day would bring.

When they got to school, they couldn't wait to go inside. They had a new teacher to meet, new friends to make, and new things to learn.

The nephews introduced themselves to the other students and their teacher.

"I'm Huey!"

"And I'm Dewey!"

"My name's Louie!"

After everyone else said hello, they found their seats and started the first lesson of the day.

Later on, after lunch and math, it was time for Huey's favorite class of the day . . . art!
Huey painted something red—the color of his shirt. "School is so fun!" he said.
"Totally!" his brothers agreed.

Next was Dewey's favorite class—language arts! He really liked learning, and his teacher was nice.

After school, they took the school bus back to Uncle Donald's house.

"I can't wait to tell Uncle Donald all about our day!" Dewey said.

"It was all so fun I can't even pick a favorite class!" Louie said.

"Uncle Donald! Uncle Donald!" they cheered as they ran through the door. "We're ready for our *second* day of school!"

But Donald was asleep. It's hard work getting three kids ready for school!

Are you ready to go to school?

Fill in the blanks below and use the handy checklist to make sure! You can also use the stickers to write your name on all your favorite school supplies, like lunch boxes, pencil cases, notebooks, and more. And if you need help, ask a pal. As Huey, Dewey, and Louie say, going back to school is fun!

My name is _____.

I wake up at _____ o'clock.

The school I go to is _____.

The grade I am in is _____.

My teacher's name is _____.

My principal's name is _____.

My favorite class is _____.

My favorite snack is _____

My best friend's name is _____

Some of my new friends are named _____
_____

My school day ends at _____ o'clock.

After school, I like to _____
_____

I can't wait to _____
tomorrow!

BACK-TO-SCHOOL PLAN

- ☐ Go for a yearly checkup at the doctor's office.
- ☐ Buy or make healthy snacks.
- ☐ Get school supplies, like folders and notebooks.
- ☐ Label all your supplies with your name.
- ☐ Learn the school rules.
- ☐ Pick out your outfit for your first day.
- ☐ Pack your backpack.
- ☐ Learn your route to school.
- ☐ Have a great school year!

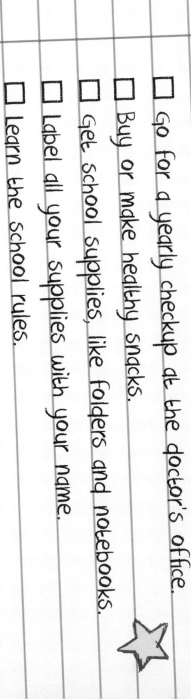